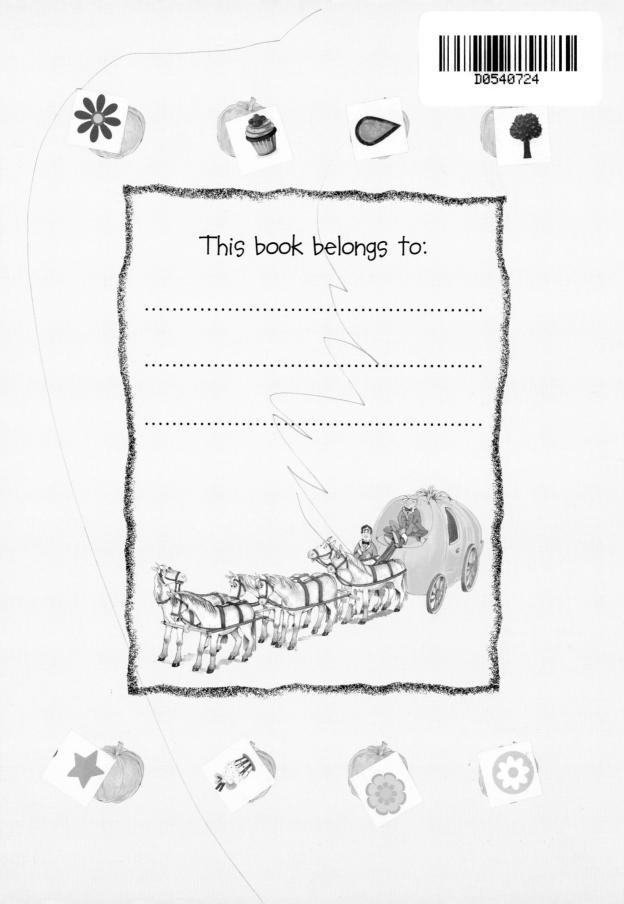

This book belongs to:

....

....

....

Retold by Gaby Goldsack
Illustrated by Kim Blundell

Language consultant: Betty Root

This edition published by Parragon in 2010

Parragon
Queen Street House
4 Queen Street
Bath BA1 1HE, UK

ISBN 978-1-4075-8918-3

Printed in China

Please retain this information for future reference

Cinderella

Bath • New York • Singapore • Hong Kong • Cologne • Delhi
Melbourne • Amsterdam • Johannesburg • Auckland • Shenzhen

Helping Your Child to Read

Learning to read is an exciting challenge for most children. From a very early age, sharing story books with children, talking about the pictures and guessing what might happen next are all very important parts of the reading experience.

Sharing reading

Set aside a regular quiet time to share reading with younger children, or to be on hand to encourage older children as they develop into independent readers.

My First Fairytales are intended to encourage and support the early stages of learning to read. They present well-loved tales that children will happily listen to again and again. Familiarity helps children to identify some of the words and phrases.

When you feel your child is ready to move on a little, encourage him or her to join in so that you read the story aloud together. Always pause to talk about the pictures. The easy-to-read speech bubbles in **My First Fairytales** provide an excellent 'joining-in' activity. The bright, clear illustrations and matching text will help children to understand the story.

Building confidence

In time, children will want to to read *to* you. When this happens, be patient and give continual praise. They may not read all the words correctly, but children's substitutions are often very good guesses.

The repetition in each book is particularly helpful for building confidence. If your child cannot read a particular word, go back to the beginning of the sentence and read it together so the meaning is not lost. Most importantly, do not continue if your child is tired or simply in need of a change.

Reading alone

The next step is to ask your child to read alone. Try to be on hand to give help and support. Remember to give lots of encouragement and praise.

Together with other simple stories, **My First Fairytales** will ensure that children will find reading an enjoyable and rewarding experience.

Once upon a time, there was a pretty
girl called Cinderella. She lived with her
stepmother and two ugly stepsisters. The
ugly stepsisters did not like Cinderella.
They made Cinderella do all the work.

One day, a card came from the Prince. There was to be a ball. Every girl in the land could go. But the stepsisters did not want Cinderella to go.

The stepsisters told Cinderella she could not go to the ball. She only had rags to wear. Cinderella was very sad.

Cinderella helped her sisters to get ready for the ball.

She helped them dress.

Help me dress, Cinderella!

Brush my hair, Cinderella!

She brushed their hair.
She tried very hard to
make them look pretty.
But it was no good.
They were just
too ugly.

The stepsisters went to the ball.

Cinderella was very sad.

She wanted to see the prince.

She sat by the fire and cried.

"Don't cry," said a voice.

It was Cinderella's fairy godmother.

"You will go to the ball," said the

fairy godmother.

You will go to the ball!

"Go and get a pumpkin," said the
fairy godmother.
Cinderella got the pumpkin.

"Go and get six
white mice," said the
fairy godmother.
Cinderella got
six white mice.

"Go and get two rats," said the
fairy godmother.

Cinderella got two rats.

"Go and get a frog," said the
fairy godmother.

Cinderella got a frog.

Ribbit!

The fairy godmother waved her
magic wand.

The pumpkin turned into a coach.

The mice turned into horses.

The two rats turned into footmen.

The frog turned into a driver.

It's magic!

The fairy godmother waved her
magic wand again.
Cinderella's dress turned into a
pretty ball gown.

Cinderella got into the coach.
"Be home before the clock strikes
midnight," said the fairy godmother.
"The magic ends at midnight."

At the ball, Cinderella saw the prince.
"Please dance with me," said the prince.
They danced all evening. The ugly sisters
did not know that the pretty girl
was Cinderella.

The clock struck midnight. Cinderella said, "I must go home!" "Come back!" said the prince.

Bong!

Bong!

Come back!

22

But Cinderella ran away.

She lost her shoe.

The prince picked it up.

The coach turned back into a pumpkin.

Cinderella's pretty ball gown turned
back into rags.

Cinderella ran all the way home.

I must go!

It's mine!

Let me try!

The next day,
the prince looked
for Cinderella.
Every girl in the land
tried on the lost shoe.
It would not fit.

Cinderella's stepsisters tried on the shoe.
It would not fit.

At last, Cinderella tried on the shoe.

It did fit!

"Will you marry me?" said the prince.

"Yes!" said Cinderella.

And so they were married and lived

happily ever after.

Read and Say

How many of these words can you say? The pictures will help you. Look back in your book and see if you can find the words in the story.

coach

clock

fairy godmother

footman

frog

gown

mice

pumpkin

prince

stepsisters

Titles in this series:

Cinderella
Goldilocks and the Three Bears
Little Red Riding Hood
The Three Billy Goats Gruff